Contents

Maximus and the Computer Mouse

One of the things that I often get asked as I visit schools is how Maximus got his name. To me he was a super-mouse, a special mouse, in fact a Maxi-Mouse. The first book of his adventures was published in 1991 and he hasn't really changed very much since then. He still gets into trouble, he still gets things wrong and he still manages somehow to land on his paws at the end of it. But those of you who know Maximus wouldn't really expect anything else.

Maximus is rather proud of the fact that you can now see him in four great colour books. These books each have one story but full colour illustrations by Elke Counsell on every page and are published by Scripture Union.

Another question I get asked is where ideas come from for the stories. Many come from the children I talk to in schools. I would especially like to thank David from Dewhurst St Mary School in Cheshunt for the idea of the story called 'Finders aren't keepers'.

As always, I love getting letters and pictures from readers and am very grateful to all those who have written to me. I hope and pray that you will enjoy these stories whether you hear them at school or read them at home.

Maximus, Patrick, Paula, the mouselings and all the others join me in sending you our very best wishes. We dedicate this book to you.

Brian Ogden

Maximus in charge

'Are you sure you're going to be all right?' asked Paula. 'I mean, they can be a bit of a pawful.'

'Paula dear,' said Maximus, 'I know I'm an old bachelor mouse, but it's only a matter of common sense, looking after mouselings.'

Patrick and Paula had come to see Maximus the day before.

'We have just heard that Paula's mother is quite poorly. We want to ask you a big favour. Would you look after the children if we go away for one night?'

Maximus had thought for a moment and scratched his whiskers. He knew all the mouselings and he was sure he could manage it. 'Of course,' he had replied, 'you must go. I shall enjoy looking after them.'

Paula began to have second thoughts as she packed the next morning. Could Maximus really keep an eye on thirty-four children? She spoke to the mouselings and made them promise to be good. 'Uncle Maximus will look after you but you must be helpful.'

Patrick and Paula turned and waved their paws as they left the Sunday School cupboard. The mouselings waved back until their parents were out of sight.

'Right, tonight is party time,' whispered Peregrine. 'Uncle Max'll be asleep by half past eight. Then we party!'

'But Mum said we must be good,' said Petronella.

'Kid sisters! Who needs kid sisters?' said Peregrine. 'Uncle Max'll never know. By the time he wakes up everything will be tidy again.'

By eight o'clock all the mouselings had got into their night-clothes and one by one came to say 'good night' to Maximus. After they had gone he turned on the television and settled down in Patrick's chair.

'Can't imagine what Paula was worried about,' Maximus said to himself. In a few minutes he was sound asleep and making little mousy snoring noises. Twenty minutes later, Peregrine tip-pawed into the lounge. He had one look at Maximus and scampered back to the other mouselings who had been lying in their beds pretending to be asleep.

'Uncle Max is in dreamland,' he said. 'Let's party.'

They jumped out of bed and crept past the lounge where Maximus was still snoring. They left the Sunday School cupboard and went into the vestry where Maximus lived.

Soon they were having a really great party. They drank flower-dew cola and ate worm-flavoured crisps. They danced and sang. They played games like postmice's knock and hide-and-squeak. It wasn't until the church clock struck midnight that they stopped.

'What about tidying up?' asked Petronella.

'I'm too tired now,' yawned Peregrine. 'We'll do it in the morning.'

The mouselings tip-pawed back to their beds in the Sunday School cupboard. Maximus was still fast asleep in front of the television.

Maximus woke as the church clock struck seven. He had a wash and then looked in his case for some clean socks. It seemed that he had packed everything apart from them. He decided to pop back to the vestry.

Maximus could not believe his eyes! His clean and tidy home looked like a rubbish tip. There were crisp packets everywhere. Empty bottles of flower-dew cola lay around the floor. The furniture was all piled in one corner. Balloons floated around in the draught from an open window. One went off like a bomb as it landed on a sharp splinter.

Maximus went slowly back to the Sunday School cupboard. If this was what mouselings did, he thought, then it wasn't much fun being a parent! It was still quiet in the cupboard when he got back. The church clock struck eight and Maximus realised that they had over-slept. Now they were going to be late for school!

Maximus rushed around trying to wake the mouselings and get the breakfast at the same time. There was a fight outside the bathroom as they all tried to get in at once. A milk bottle was knocked over as they scrambled for the cereal. Half of them couldn't find their school clothes, four told Maximus they had P.E. that morning and needed their shorts, and six of the older ones couldn't find their homework.

'Mrs Whiskers'll kill us,' said Petunia, Petronella, Primrose and Pauline. 'She told us we must have our projects in today. Will you write us a note? Please, Uncle Max?'

'I don't like porridge,' sobbed Paulinus, 'it's got funny bits in it.'

Maximus didn't have time to speak to any of the mouselings about the vestry before they scampered off.

'Can we have cheese pie for tea, please, Uncle Maximus?' said Percival and Pilbright.

Maximus was exhausted. Perhaps it wasn't very easy being a parent after all. How did Patrick and Paula manage it? There was still the vestry to sort out and now the mouselings wanted cheese pie.

7

Maximus had cooked cheese pie for himself but he didn't think he could cook it for thirty-four hungry mouselings. Then he had a dreadful thought. The bedroom. How had they left the bedroom? Probably like the vestry.

Maximus hardly dared look. When he opened the door it was worse than he expected. No beds were made. No pyjamas had been put away. None of yesterday's clothes were put out for washing.

Maximus tottered into the lounge and dropped down into Patrick's chair. In a few seconds he was fast asleep. He didn't hear the door open. He didn't wake up when Patrick and Paula walked in. He didn't hear them tidy the bedroom or begin to cook supper for the mouselings. In fact, he didn't wake up until Patrick brought him a cup of tea.

'The children will be home soon,' said Patrick. 'How have you got on?'

'Well,' said Maximus, 'I didn't realise that it was such hard work being a parent. I really don't know how you and Paula manage it. Things have got in rather a mess.'

Maximus decided not to tell Patrick and Paula about the vestry. He went home and, just as he was starting to clear it up, Peregrine and some of the other mouselings came in.

'We're really sorry, Uncle Max,' they said. 'We've come to help.'

And Maximus thought – it may be hard being a parent but you can forgive mouselings most things.

Heavenly Father,
Thank you for our parents and for all who look after us. Help us to think about them and to be helpful and not careless, to be kind and not unthinking, to be loving and not selfish. Amen.

9

The Open University

Maximus stood waiting by the vestry door. Why was it that when he wanted something to come the post was always late? At that moment a large brown envelope fell through the letterbox. Maximus tore it open and read the following letter.

Dear Mr Maximus Mouse,

Thank you for your letter and for returning your application form for Mousebridge Open University. I am pleased to inform you that you have been accepted as a student on the Creative Writing Course.

I shall be your tutor for the Course. Please complete the first piece of written work and return it to me by the end of the month.

May I take this opportunity to wish you well for all your studies.

Yours sincerely,

Professor William Shakepaw

Maximus rushed out of the vestry and over to the Sunday School cupboard. 'Patrick,' he shouted, 'it's come. I've had a letter from Professor Shakepaw. I'm a student of Mousebridge Open University.'

Patrick waved his brown envelope at Maximus. 'Mine's come too. We've both been accepted.'

The two mice had talked about becoming students for ages and finally Paula, who was tired of them both, told them to apply.

'Now you can show the mouselings what hard work is really like,' she said. 'Why don't you make a start on your first project?'

'*Write a short poem about being a mouse,*' read Maximus. '*You must imagine that it will be read by a human who has no idea how a mouse feels.*'

They sat for a long time gazing at the blank sheets of white paper in front of them. Maximus chewed the end of his pencil and Patrick started to nibble the paper. At last they both started writing. Patrick put his paw in front of his poem so that Maximus couldn't see it.

'Read it to me, Pat,' said Maximus. 'Go on, please.'

Patrick coughed and started to read.

'*Mice* by Patrick Mouse.

I have always been a mouse,
I was born a mouse in my mother's house.
I have mousy hair and a mousy tail,
And I'm really glad I'm not a whale.

I think mousy thoughts, both day and night,
If I see a cat I have a mousy fright.
My wife is a mousy wife –
And I shall stay a mouse all my life.'

'That's brilliant,' said Maximus. 'Now let me read you mine.'

11

'*Maximus Mouse* by Maximus Mouse

I have known me all my life,
From the day that I was born.
I have never been anyone else –
From dawn to dawn to dawn.

A mouse I am, a mouse I shall stay,
Whatever anyone does or whatever they may say.
From tip of my nose to end of my tail –
I am mouse all the way through, without fail.'

'Amazing,' said Patrick, 'just amazing. We've written our first poems. That Professor Shakepaw will be so pleased with us.'

'We might win a prize with these poems,' said Maximus. 'I'm sure when he sees how clever we are he won't expect us to write any more. Come on, let's put them in the post.'

Patrick and Maximus scampered off to the pillar-box and posted their work back to Professor Shakepaw. A week later they got replies.

Dear Mr Maximus,

Thank you for sending me your poem entitled 'Maximus Mouse by Maximus Mouse'. *I regret to say that this is of a very poor standard and I seriously question whether you should continue with the Course. This University takes its Creative Writing standards very seriously, which is more than you appear to have done, with the absurd poem you submitted. I can only assume that it was intended as a misplaced joke.*

I am prepared to give you one more chance. Your assignment is to write a poem to describe the finest

12

cheddar cheese you have ever eaten.

I have written to Mr Patrick Mouse along similar lines as it appears that you consult one another over your work. I hope there will be an immediate improvement in your work.

Yours sincerely,

Professor William Shakepaw

Maximus, for once in his life, was squeakless. He could not believe that anyone could write to him like that. Well, that was it – there was not going to be any more. Professor Shakepaw could find other students. He was obviously a man who simply did not recognise good poetry when he saw it.

At that moment Patrick came into the vestry carrying his copy of the letter from Professor Shakepaw.

'I don't think he liked it!' said Patrick.

'He didn't,' shouted Maximus. 'And I don't like him! I'm not wasting my time writing poetry for him any more.'

'I feel the same,' said Patrick, 'but Paula thinks we should try again. She says now we can only get better. She said something about how it's easy to give up but much harder to carry on. She did also say something about us setting an example to the mouselings.'

'She's a hard mouse, that wife of yours,' said Maximus. 'I mean, how would she feel if it had happened to her?'

'Well, I'm going to try again,' said Patrick. 'Why don't you do the same?'

'I'll think about it,' said Maximus. Patrick went back home to the Sunday School cupboard and Maximus threw himself onto his duvet.

By the next morning he had calmed down. Perhaps

his poetry wasn't brilliant after all. Perhaps he did need some help. Perhaps he could do better. He sat down and tried again. This time he thought about what he wanted to write. He wrote it down, read it through and then wrote it again. He did this twice until he was really sure he had written it as well as he could.

Maximus and Patrick put their new poems in the post to Professor Shakepaw without reading each other's work. It took another week before the Professor replied. Maximus tore open the envelope and read the following words:

Dear Mr Maximus Mouse,

I can hardly believe that you are the same student who wrote the poem 'Maximus Mouse'. Your poem about favourite cheddar cheese shows great improvement and I shall be publishing it in the U.S.A. at the end of term.

Congratulations and keep up the good work.

Yours sincerely,

Professor William Shakepaw.

P.S. U.S.A. stands for University Students' Anthology.

Maximus went to supper that evening with Patrick and Paula. The professor had also been pleased with Patrick's poem.

'You see, it only goes to show, you can do things if you put some effort into it,' said Paula. 'Now, Maximus, you must read me your poem.'

And this is the poem that Maximus read:

'Cheddar Cheese and the Five Senses

To smell, and taste, and then to touch,
To hear and see, it is too much,
When thinking of that rare delight –
A piece of cheddar cheese tonight.

The smell is finer than perfume,
Than any rose that is in bloom;
The taste puts chocolate in the shade –
It's worth however much you paid.

The silky touch when paw meets cheese,
Is guaranteed to more than please;
O listen as it speaks to you
Of quality that's always true.

To see it, is the greatest pleasure,
To regard it at my leisure –
And let my senses dwell at ease
Upon my favourite Cheddar Cheese.'

Heavenly Father,
Help us to understand that everything we do must be
the best we can do. In our work at school, in the
games we play and in our love for you, help us to give
only the best. Amen.

16

The lost mouseling

Maximus lay in the sort of doze when you are half awake and half asleep. Suddenly a thought came to him. He leapt out of bed, fell over his slippers, picked himself up and rushed out into the church.

'It's the day,' he shouted. 'The special day we've all been waiting for.'

He scampered to the Sunday School cupboard. Paula came to the door.

'It's today,' he said. 'Why aren't you ready?'

'What is the matter, Maximus? Why are you jumping around in the church in your pyjamas? What's all this shouting about?'

'But it's your special day, Paula,' said Maximus. 'It's your wedding anniversary.' He rushed over to Paula, clutching his pyjama trousers as he ran, and gave her a big kiss.

'Maximus, what would the children say?' said Paula, rather breathlessly. 'Here you are, half naked, squeezing the squeak out of me, and generally making a nuisance of yourself.'

Maximus stood there with his paws behind his back, one paw holding his pyjama trousers tightly. But Paula hadn't finished.

'Go and get dressed,' she continued, 'and by the time you're ready we'll be waiting for you.' And with that she

18

turned round and went back into the cupboard from which Maximus heard a lot of tiny squeaks.

Half an hour later, dressed in his best going-to-picnic jeans and M-shirt, Maximus knocked on the cupboard door again. The door opened and Maximus took several steps backwards. There, in front of him, was the whole of Patrick and Paula's family – thirty-four mouselings.

'Good morning, Uncle Maximus,' they chorused together.

'Er... good morning,' answered Maximus. 'Are you ready for the picnic?'

'Yes, Uncle Maximus,' they said.

Maximus could never understand how it was that Patrick and Paula knew all their children. Thirty-four seemed so many. How did they remember their names? Did they know all their birthdays? How did they tell which shoes belonged to which paws? It was all quite beyond Maximus.

The mouselings crowded round Maximus, all trying to be the one who held his paw. Soon their parents had sorted them out so that the older children looked after the younger ones. They made a long procession, walking out of the church and into the churchyard.

It was a beautiful spring day and the children scampered off, running around the gravestones, playing hide-and-squeak, mouse tag and other games.

'Well, you've got a lovely day for your anniversary,' said Maximus to Patrick and Paula. The three grown-up mice lay in the sunshine. 'It's really great to relax and chat to old friends like this.'

After an hour or so they began to feel hungry.

'Nearly time for lunch,' said Paula. 'Patrick, I think you should start to get the children together. Make sure they wash their paws in that puddle before they sit down.' Paula began to unpack a large bag of tiny cheese burgers and worm-paste sandwiches. Maximus could hear Patrick counting the mouselings.

'Twenty-eight, twenty-nine... Peregrine, do stand still, thirty, thirty-one... Pomegranate, put Prudence down... thirty-two, thirty-three, er... where is thirty-four? Has anyone seen Percival?' asked Patrick anxiously. But none of the others had seen him anywhere.

'It would be Percy. He really is the limit. He never does what he's told,' joined in Paula. 'If any mouseling is going to get lost, it will always be Percy.'

'Patrick, you and I will search,' said Maximus, 'while the others stay with Paula.'

Patrick and Maximus set off through the long grass which grew between some of the older gravestones. Maximus scrambled up on top of one of them but he couldn't see the missing mouseling. They scampered on a little further and shouted again. There was no answer. Patrick was looking very worried and Maximus tried to comfort him.

'I'm sure we'll find Percy soon,' he said. 'He's really quite a sensible mouse – he can't be far away.'

'I do hope you're right,' said Patrick, 'there are so many things that can happen to young mice today. He might have been mousenapped or caught by a cat or even run over.'

'Shush! I mean... listen for a moment. I thought I heard a squeak. It's coming from over there.' Maximus pointed towards the rubbish dump near the churchyard fence. It was full of rotting grass from the mower, stumps of old flowers were sticking out like gelled hair, and the smell was terrible. They held their paws to their noses as they started to climb over the rubbish.

'Percival,' shouted Patrick, 'Percy, are you there?'

They listened hard for a reply. There was a tiny squeak.

'Dad, Dad... I'm down here. Please get me out.'

It took Patrick and Maximus quite a long time to move all the leaves and twigs to rescue Percy. At last he was free. Before they scampered back to a very worried Paula, Patrick spoke to his son.

'Percy, you were very naughty to go off on your own. You know we always tell you to stay near us. Your mother is worried out of her fur.'

'Dad, I'm really sorry. I was ever so scared under all those things. I couldn't move. But I knew you would look for me. I just knew you would come.'

The three of them went back to join the others.

'Come on everyone, we've found Percy so let's celebrate,' said Maximus. All the mouselings joined in and they had a fantastic party. They were so happy that the mouseling that was lost had been found.

Next Sunday, Maximus sat in church during the Family Service hoping one of the choir boys would drop a piece of chocolate. Maximus started to take notice when the vicar read the lesson from the Bible. It was the story Jesus told about a lost sheep. A shepherd has a hundred sheep and loses one of them. He searches for it until he finds it. He is so happy when he finds it that he has a party.

'God is happy, like that shepherd,' said the vicar, 'when someone who has done wrong tells God he is sorry and asks to be forgiven.'

'I think I know a little bit how it feels,' thought Maximus. 'We felt the same when Percy was found.'

Dear God,
Sometimes we feel a long way away from you. Help us to remember that you are always there with us. Forgive us for the things we do that make you unhappy. Amen.

The mouse with the longest tail

Maximus came back from shopping and could not believe what had happened in his vestry. It had been invaded. One of the old cupboards had gone and in its place was a sort of desk.

The desk had three shelves. On the top one there seemed to be a television. On the next shelf was a flat box with lots of little letters and numbers. The letters weren't in order like A B C D. They started Q W E R T Y. And then on the third shelf down was a larger box holding pieces of paper.

Usually Maximus only saw the vicar a few times each week but after the arrival of the box he seemed to come more often. Maximus hid behind the curtains on the window-sill and watched what the vicar did. He sat at the desk and pushed a switch. The television made lots of funny noises – whirrs and buzzes and hiccoughs and then nothing much happened. The programmes on the television were very boring – all letters and numbers. The vicar didn't seem to know what he was doing and sometimes got quite cross with the television.

One day two of the choir boys came into the vestry with the vicar.

'Well, I hope you two can tell me what's wrong,' said the vicar. 'I'm not very good with these things.'

'I think what you need,' said David, one of the

choirboys, 'is a new mouse.'

Maximus, who was on the window-sill again, nearly fell on the floor.

'A new mouse?' he said to himself. 'Excuse me, but there's nothing wrong with me. I'm a perfectly good mouse. I come highly recommended – by me.'

'And will this new mouse be expensive?' asked the vicar. 'I can't afford to spend too much at the moment.'

'They cost about twenty pounds,' said Jason, David's friend. 'You can get them in Hurry's or Mickson's.'

Maximus thought he was hearing things – Hurry's and Mickson's weren't pet shops. Something was badly wrong. Whatever was the vicar thinking of?

'Well, if that's what I need,' said the vicar, 'then that's what I shall have to get – a new mouse. I'll get it while I'm out tomorrow. I'll throw the old one away when I get the new one.'

As soon as the vicar and the choirboys had left the vestry Maximus scampered over to see Patrick and Paula.

'I've been made rodent-dunded,' he shouted. 'The vicar doesn't want me any more. He's going to buy a new mouse and throw me away.'

'Calm down, Maximus,' said Paula gently. 'I'm sure it can't be as bad as that. I'll make us a nice cup of nettle tea.'

'Come and sit down, Maximus,' said Patrick, 'and tell me exactly what you heard.'

Maximus told them how the vicar had brought the television set and other bits and pieces into the vestry, how the vicar wasn't very good at making it work and had needed the choirboys to help him and then how the boys had told him he needed a new mouse.

'He probably needs a mouse who understands all these things. One who can get into the television and make it work again,' said Maximus. 'I was never any good at science at school.'

'I think what we had better do,' said Patrick thoughtfully, 'is to have a look at these things when the vicar won't be there. I'll come over to the vestry at midnight.'

'I think you should come and help me pack,' said Maximus. 'I shall have to find somewhere else to live when they throw me away.'

Just as the church clock struck twelve, the moon broke free from the cloud that had been hiding her from the earth. Patrick scampered across the church and ran into the vestry. Maximus was still dressed and sat, looking very miserable, on his duvet.

Bravely the two mice climbed to the top of the new desk and stood by the television. At that moment the moon shone brightly through the vestry window. Patrick found a knob on the side of the screen and pushed it. The machine whirred and buzzed and hiccoughed. The two mice clung tightly to each other until the noise stopped. Suddenly there was a lot of light from the screen and some words appeared.

Patrick read the words.

'WELCOME TO DOORS 97.
USE THE MOUSE TO POINT TO
THE PROGRAMME YOU WANT.'

'You see,' said Maximus, 'they don't think I can point. They want to throw me away and get a new mouse!'

'Hold on, Maximus,' said Patrick, 'I think I know what this is. It isn't a television – it's a computer. The vicar wants to use it for writing letters and keeping church records and lots of things like that.'

'But what about the mouse?' asked Maximus. 'What does the mouse do that I can't?'

'I think if we follow this tail we might find the answer,' said Patrick.

Coming out of the back of the computer was what looked to the two mice like a long tail. They followed it round the back of the computer and along the edge of the desk until they came to a small mat. Sitting on the mat, at the end of the tail, was what looked in the moonlight like a funny shaped mouse.

Maximus did his best to growl – not something mice are very good at. Patrick tried not to laugh.

'Er... Maximus,' he said, 'this is what is called a computer mouse. He lives on this mouse mat and his tail goes into the computer. When you move him about, an arrow shows on the computer screen. I've seen them in Hurry's and Mickson's. They are very clever with computers but no good for anything else.'

'Oh dear,' said Maximus, 'I seem to have got it wrong again. Perhaps the vicar doesn't want to throw me out after all. I might try to get to know the new mouse.'

'And Maximus, do be careful when you overhear people talking – it might not be about you!' said Patrick.

Loving Father,
There are times when we don't understand what people are talking about and we get things wrong. We worry about it and get cross.

Help us to trust and believe that you always know what is best for us and will look after us at all times. Amen.

Sandcastles should be built on rocks

'Just what we wanted,' said Patrick. 'The tide's out and there's lots of sand for the mouselings to play on.'

Maximus, Patrick, Paula and the mouselings had just arrived at the seaside and they were walking along the promenade.

'Right,' ordered Paula, 'down on the beach. Make sure all your shoes and socks are left tidily. We shall have a swim this afternoon when our lunch has gone down. Older ones, please look after younger ones. And Percival, I shall be watching you. One paw out of line and no ice cream!'

The mouselings started to dig in the sand. Prunella and Pomegranate, together with Peregrine and Percival, wandered down towards the sea.

'We can make a bigger castle than you,' boasted Percy. 'I mean, you're only girl mice!'

Prunella and Pomegranate looked at each other, then nodded their heads.

'You're on,' said Prunella. 'We'll have a competition.'

'Right,' said Peregrine, 'if yours is biggest, you can have our ices but if ours is best...'

'Which it will be,' said Percy.

'... we will have yours.'

Both pairs started to dig quickly. The girl mouselings chose a spot where a small flat-topped rock jutted up out of the sand. The boys went nearer to the edge of the sea where the sand was wetter and stuck together better. They all worked very hard. They filled their buckets, tipped them out, built up the sand walls and then did it all again.

'Can't wait for TWO ice creams,' said Percy, loud enough for the girls to hear. 'Look at yours!' he said, pointing to the girls' castle. 'Have you started yet?'

The girls ignored Percy's question and carried on with their work.

'Right,' said Pomegranate, 'half an hour more, then we'll get Uncle Maximus and Mum and Dad to judge which is best.'

'Shouldn't bother,' said Peregrine, ''sobvious. Ours is best.'

Both pairs worked even harder. Buckets were filled and emptied. The castles got higher and higher. The mouselings got hotter and hotter. The boys had flung off their M-shirts which were now lying in a little rock pool being nibbled by crabs. The one thing that nobody noticed was that the tide was slowly creeping up the beach.

As the last bucket of sand slid off their castle and onto the beach the boys shouted out, 'Finished. Time's up. We've won!'

It certainly looked as though the boys' castle was higher than the girls'. Peregrine and Percy jumped around punching the air with their paws and shouting 'Yes!'

Percy ran off to find Maximus and his parents.

'Come quick,' he said to them.

'Quickly, dear... we say "come quickly", not "come quick",' corrected Paula as Percy tumbled into a deep hole dug by Popsie and Posie. 'What's the matter? Are Prunella and Pomegranate all right?'

'Yes, fine, Mum, we're all fine,' said Percival. 'We want you three to come and judge our complication.'

'I think you mean "competition",' said Maximus with a grin. 'What sort of competition is it?'

'We, that is me and Percy, bet the girls we could make a bigger castle than them. If we win we get their ice creams!'

Maximus, Patrick and Paula followed Percy over the beach, dotted with little holes dug by the rest of the family, towards the two castles. Percy was dancing around them and soon Peregrine joined in.

'So we have to judge which castle is the highest, do we?' asked Maximus.

'Yes, Uncle Maximus, but we're the best,' shouted the two boy mouselings together.

The adult mice went over to look at the castle built by Pomegranate and Prunella. It was spread well over the little rock and looked very strong. There were flags on each corner and it was about three buckets high.

'Well done,' said Paula. 'You've worked very hard but now let's have a look at the boys' castle.'

Suddenly Percy gave a loud scream. The adults turned round just in time. A wave broke over the boys' castle and knocked it flat. It was as if it had never been there. The beach was as flat as it had been before they started.

They all sang in the coach going home – apart, that is, from Percival and Peregrine who were not happy mouselings.

The next Sunday morning Maximus was, as usual, in church. Just as he had found a cough sweet stuck to the floor under the organist's stool he heard the vicar reading from the Bible.

'"*Anyone who hears these words of mine,*" said Jesus, "*and obeys them, is like a wise man who built*

30

his house on a rock. " The words of Jesus are like a rock in a stormy sea,' the vicar went on. 'Whatever happens to us, if we cling to those words, we shall never fall. It's a bit like building two sandcastles – one on a rock and one on the beach and watching what happens when the tide comes in.'

'I know what you mean,' whispered Maximus to himself.

Heavenly Father,
Thank you for the stories which Jesus told. Help us to understand his words and to obey them at all times so that our lives might be built on the rock which is Jesus. Amen.

The prodigal mouseling

'Go on, Uncle Maximus. Please tell us a story,' begged the mouselings.

'Tell us a story about when you were a mouseling,' said Percy. 'What was it like in the old days?'

'Less of the old days!' said Maximus with a smile.

Maximus was mouseling-sitting as Patrick and Paula had gone out to the mouselings' school.

'Once upon a time,' said Maximus, 'I did a very silly thing. My brothers and sisters and I lived with our parents in a very nice mouse hole in a farmhouse. Of course there were the usual problems. The farm cat was what humans call a very good mouser.'

'Did that mean she was kind to mice?' asked Posie.

'No,' said Percy, 'it means she...'

'... it means that the cat was very unkind to us mice,' said Maximus, just managing to interrupt Percy.

'But most of the time,' said Maximus, continuing his story, 'we had a very good life. Living on a farm there was always lots of food. But as I got older I began to get bored. Every day seemed the same as the last one. I began to hear stories from other mice who came on holiday to the farm. They told me about life in the town.'

'Wish we could have a holiday in a town,' whispered Peregrine.

'It sounded great,' Maximus went on, 'lots of big shops, a football team, a zoo and a cinema. It seemed much more exciting than staying on the farm with the rest of the family. One day I told my mum and dad I was leaving. I asked for my pocket money for the rest of the month, packed my mouse coat, and left. I could see they were very sad but they didn't stop me. I managed to jump on a van that had brought things to the farm and when the van stopped an hour later I was in the town.'

'Brilliant!' said Percy loudly.

'Yes, it was, for a few days,' said Maximus. 'I soon made friends when they saw I had money to spend. But the friends went when the money went. By the end of the week I hadn't got any money and I hadn't got any friends either. I was hungry and lonely in a big town.'

'That wasn't very nice, Uncle Maximus,' said Petronella. 'Whatever did you do?'

'Well,' said Maximus thoughtfully, 'I tried to get a job but nobody had any work for a country mouse. It was then I started to think about home – about Mum and Dad back on the farm, about my brothers and sisters. I was really ashamed of what I had done. The next day I tried to find the same van that had brought me to the town. But it was no use – I just had to walk.'

'It must have been awful,' said Pomegranate.

'It was. Then the most wonderful thing happened,' said Maximus. 'As I got near to the farm I saw Dad. He had climbed onto the gate post and was looking for me. When he saw me he jumped down and scampered as fast as he could towards me. I... just stood still.'

'You were really in trouble then,' said Percy.

'Well, no, I wasn't, as it turned out,' said Maximus. 'My father was so pleased to see me. He hugged me and took me back to the mouse hole where my mother gave me a huge hug too.'

34

'You mean they forgave you for running off like that?' said Peregrine.

'They did,' said Maximus. 'In fact they not only forgave me but they had a big party as well. Dad told me that if you love someone enough you can forgive them anything. I've never forgotten that.'

'Wow,' said Percy, 'that was some story!'

'And now, young mouselings, off to bed,' said Maximus, 'before your parents come home.'

The next Sunday morning the mouselings were in the Sunday School cupboard listening to the story the Sunday School teacher was telling the children.

'Jesus told a story,' she said, 'about a young man who asked his father for his share of the family's money. The young man went off and spent it...'

'We've heard this before,' said Percy. 'It's just like the story Uncle Maximus told us.'

'I wonder if it ends the same way?' asked Petronella. 'Can humans forgive each other like we mice do?'

'... And the father was so pleased to see him,' continued the teacher, 'that he forgave his son and they all had a party. Jesus told that story so we should know that God is just like that. God loves us so much, that when we do something wrong, he will forgive us when we are really sorry.'

And the mouselings were very quiet as the teacher ended her story.

Heavenly Father,
Thank you for the story about the loving father. Help us to remember that you are always there for us —
whether we have done right or done wrong. Thank you that your love is so great that you will forgive our wrong doings if we are truly sorry. Amen.

Unexpected visitors: Christmas

It was Christmas Eve and Maximus couldn't remember a colder Christmas. The wind was blowing hard against the vestry windows and there were flakes of snow in the wind. It was bitterly cold even though the heating was on for the Christmas Day services. Maximus had given his presents to Patrick, Paula and the mouselings. He had sent cards to Barnabas the church bat, to Herbert the hedgehog, and to Robert and his family of rabbits.

Maximus was actually feeling quite proud of himself. For once he was ready for the great day. He had done his shopping and bought all the food he would need. Usually he had Christmas lunch with Patrick and Paula but they had gone away and Maximus was on his own.

There were old films on the television – *Mousy Poppins* about a nursemouse who could do magical things, *The Snowmouse* and *Soot Black and the Seven Mouselings*. He had seen them all before.

'Might as well go to bed,' he said to the empty vestry. 'Then when I wake up I can open my pressies. But it's going to be a lonely Christmas on my own.'

Maximus snuggled down under his duvet. He had managed to find several tissues and a real handkerchief so his bed was really warm and comfortable. Very soon he was asleep and snoring quietly.

Half an hour later there was a strange noise. It

sounded as though somebody was trying to get into the vestry through Maximus' special hole. At first the noise didn't wake Maximus but as it got louder he stirred.

Suddenly he was wide awake. There was definitely somebody in his vestry. He lay quite still on his bed and listened hard. There were two somebodies – he could hear them whispering. Were they burglars after his Christmas presents? Was he was going to be mouse-napped and held to ransom?

After ten minutes he could stand it no longer. They were still there and he had to know what they were doing. He got up very quietly and found the little torch he kept under the bed. He turned it on and shone the beam round the vestry.

There on the carpet by the vicar's desk, holding their paws in front of their eyes to shield them from the light, were two strange mice. They looked very cold and very wet and very tired.

'And just what do you think you are doing?' asked Maximus, sounding braver than he felt. 'This is my vestry – you are tresmousing!'

'We're looking for somewhere to stay,' said one of the mice. 'You see, my wife is going to have mouselings very soon. We are mouseholeless and it's freezing outside. Please, please may we stay?'

Maximus scratched his head with his paw. They looked so unhappy that he couldn't throw them out.

'Yes, er ... of course. I expect you're hungry,' he went on. 'Let's see what I can find.'

He looked at his Christmas lunch of carol sheet pasta with candle wax sauce. Perhaps that would cheer them up. He soon warmed it and gave it to the visitors. He made some stinging nettle tea and sat with them as they all warmed their paws round the mugs. Maximus put his duvet gently round the lady mouse's shoulders.

'My name's Jo and my wife's name is Maria. The house we were living in was knocked down to build a new road. We've been desperately searching for somewhere to have our first mouselings.'

'It is so kind of you, er... Mr... um?' said Maria.

'Maximus,' said Maximus. 'I'm the mousekeeper in this church. I sort of keep an eye on things for the vicar.'

'Mr Maximus, it really is very good of you to let us stay.'

Maximus found some more warm things for Jo and Maria and they all settled down to sleep. It was quite late on Christmas morning before Maximus woke up again. He yawned and stretched his paws and started to think about what had happened in the night. Then he heard a funny little noise. It was the sort of tiny squeaking noise that Paula's mouselings sometimes made.

Maximus jumped out of bed and scampered over to the vicar's desk. There, in an open drawer, was a very proud looking Jo, a tired but happy Maria, and six tiny baby mouselings.

'Maximus, meet your honorary grandchildren,' said Jo with a big smile.

Maximus was squeakless. It was just amazing to see the tiny mouselings all nestling up to their mother. Their eyes were shut and they wore very little fur. Maximus' duvet was tucked around them and they seemed warm and happy.

'Well,' said Maximus, 'I just don't know what to say. It's quite a surprise to wake up to find six new mouselings in my vestry. Congratulations. Have you thought of any names yet?'

'There are two boys and four girls,' said Jo. 'We thought, if you didn't mind, we would call the oldest boy Maximus, after you, and the younger one Thomas. The girls will be named after our mothers, Susan and Sally, and after the children's grandparents, Eleanor and Patricia.'

'I should be very honoured,' said Maximus.

'I hope you weren't too lonely without us,' said Paula, when the family came home on Boxing Day.

'Yes, we thought about you being on your own,' said Patrick.

'I wasn't on my own,' said Maximus. 'I had a wonderful Christmas. You see, I had some rather unexpected visitors and they had babies and I'm an honorary grandad.'

Maximus told Patrick and Paula the whole story of how Jo and Maria had arrived and how their babies had been born in the vestry as they were homeless.

'It's very strange because that's not really the end,' said Maximus. 'Just after they had gone to look for a home of their own I went into the church. Lying on the floor under the choir stalls was a carol sheet. I was just about to eat it when some words caught my eye. They were these. They were so nice I learnt them:

Away in a manger, no crib for a bed,
The little Lord Jesus laid down his sweet head.
The stars in the bright sky looked down where he lay,
The little Lord Jesus asleep on the hay.

It sort of reminded me of what happened on Christmas Day in my vestry.'

Loving Father,
You gave us Jesus at Christmas time. Help us to know him, to love him and to serve him, every day in the year. Amen.

Pawprints in the snow

Maximus could hardly believe his eyes. The world had changed. Last night, before he went to bed, it had looked as it usually did. The grass was green. The church was grey. The trees were brown. Today everything was the same colour. Everywhere Maximus looked the world was white. It wasn't only white – it was cold as well.

Maximus couldn't remember when there had last been so much snow. Most winters there was a little, but it didn't last long and soon it went all slushy and horrible. But today was different – the snow was very deep.

As Maximus looked out of the vestry window he saw some of Patrick and Paula's mouselings come rushing out. Percy picked up some snow, made it into a ball, and threw it at Posie. Soon there was a snowball fight going on. As usual Percy and Peregrine were in the thick of it. They threw snowballs, pushed snow down their brothers' and sisters' necks, and made a slide down one of the gravestones.

It looked great fun and before much longer Maximus, Patrick and Paula were outside. The mouselings split into two snowball-throwing teams. Suddenly, from behind a large gravestone, there was a scream and then a shout.

41

'Help... help me!'

Patrick and Maximus scampered as fast as they could through the snow to where the scream had come from. There was no sign of anybody. All they could see was one small glove. Patrick picked it up.

'Posie,' he said. 'It's Posie's glove. Her name is on the label.'

'Patrick,' said Maximus, pointing to tracks in the snow, 'this is very serious. Those are not mice paw-marks – they belong to a cat. Posie has been mouse-napped!'

Patrick covered his face with his paws and stood there shaking.

'Come on,' said Maximus, 'collect the rest of the mouselings. Take them to Paula and tell her to keep them inside the church. I shall start following the tracks. You catch me up as soon as you can. Come on now, Patrick. Move!'

Patrick hurried off to round up the other mouselings. Maximus set off in pursuit of the cat. It wasn't difficult to see the pawprints in the snow. They led Maximus towards the wall which surrounded the graveyard. Just by the wall there was a very deep set of prints. It was where the cat had sprung onto the wall and over the other side.

There was no way that Maximus could jump that high and he lost some time by having to go round to the gate and then find where the cat had landed. He soon spotted it and followed the pawprints once again. They seemed to be leading along the side of a hedge towards an old barn. Johann Sebastian, the organist's cat, had told Maximus that there were some very fierce stray cats living in the barn. In fact, Johann had lost a piece of his ear in a fight with one of them.

Things were going from bad to worse, thought

Maximus. Not only had Posie been mouse-napped but it was looking as though she would be taken to the cat gang's home. How could they rescue her from there? Perhaps it would be better to just leave it at that – to go home and try and forget about Posie. After all, Patrick and Paula had lots of other mouselings. Besides which they were Patrick and Paula's children – not his. Why should *he* risk becoming cat food?

Maximus shook himself and little flakes of snow flew off. It would be easy to go back to the vestry, to get warm again, to have some lunch and put on the television. But he couldn't do it. He knew he had to try and rescue Posie. But how? For the moment all he could do was to follow.

The trail led further along the hedge and then suddenly stopped. No pawprints lay ahead. It was as if the mousenapper had just vanished. Maximus stopped. The cat could not just have disappeared. Some snow fell on his whiskers. He looked up just in time to see the cat, almost hidden in the hedge, about to spring on him. The falling snow had saved him. Maximus dived into the hedge as the cat landed on the spot where he had been only a second before.

Posie, held by the cat's teeth, fell free as the cat landed with a bump. Maximus shouted at her.

'Posie! Quick. Over here.'

Posie saw it was Maximus, and scampered under the hedge as fast as the snow would let her. The prickly hedge was really thick at its base and the cat could not get its paws on the two terrified mice. It stood there snarling and spitting at them, trying to tear away the undergrowth. Just as the last branch broke off, the mice heard a loud bark. A big black dog came running up to the hedge. The cat snarled. It turned and ran with the dog chasing after it.

43

Maximus made sure that Posie was all right. Very carefully, stopping every now and then to make sure they were not being followed, they made their way back to the church. As they got to the gate they met Patrick.

Soon they were inside and feeling safe and warm. Posie hadn't been hurt by the cat, just very frightened.

'Maximus. You were just amazing,' said Paula. 'We can't tell you how grateful we are that you rescued Posie.'

'You were so brave,' said Patrick, 'you didn't think about yourself, you just thought about Posie.'

'That's not really true,' said Maximus slowly, 'you see, I did think about me. I'm ashamed to say that I nearly turned round and came back home. I wasn't brave. I was terrified.'

'But that's being really brave,' said Paula quietly. 'When you are really terrified but you still go on – that's real courage.'

Posie crept over to Maximus, sat on his knee, and gave him a big hug.

'Uncle Maximus, you're the bravest mouse in the world,' said Posie.

Patrick and Paula tried hard not to notice the big tear falling down Maximus' cheek.

Heavenly Father,
Jesus was the bravest person who ever lived. When we need courage to do what we have to do, may we remember to ask Jesus to help us. Amen.

Finders aren't keepers

Maximus opened his purse, shook it, and waited for the sound of falling coins. There was silence. Nothing came out. It was what he was afraid of – he was broke. There was no other way to describe it.

He had been to the Sales and spent all his money. He had bought a new duvet, a CD player, and some new CDs to go with it. His favourite group was called *Hard Cheese* and their new CD was very expensive. He especially liked the track with the words:

'Eat it, beat it, meet it, Hard Cheese;
Cheat for it, bleat for it, don't ever delete it;
Hard Cheese.'

In fact he played it so often that Patrick wouldn't come into the vestry when it was on.

But all this spending had left him without any money – not even enough to buy food. Having had no breakfast and no lunch he went round to see Patrick and Paula.

'I don't suppose you could lend me some money?' he asked. 'You see, I need to go shopping, and it's sort of disappeared.'

'You mean you've spent it all,' said Paula.

'Hard Cheese!' said Patrick.

'That's not very nice,' said Maximus. 'I ask you politely if I can borrow some money and all you can say is "hard cheese".'

'Hard Cheese are the problem, Maximus,' said Patrick, with a grin. 'If you hadn't bought their CD you might have enough money to buy food.'

'I see what you mean,' said Maximus, 'but... er, I am rather hungry.'

'Of course you can borrow some,' said Paula, and she gave Maximus some coins from her purse. 'I can't lend you much. We've got to get some new shoes for the mouselings tomorrow.'

'Thanks,' said Maximus. 'I'll let you have it back as soon as I can.'

Maximus always walked through the park to the Wasda Supermarket. There was a pretty lake in the park and Maximus usually stopped and had a chat with the ducks. Today there was nobody about. No ducks, no squirrels, no moles, nobody to be seen at all. Maximus, whose tummy was beginning to rumble, scampered by the lake and headed towards the gate opposite the Supermarket.

Suddenly he stopped. Had he really seen it or had he dreamt it? No, he was right. It was there, on the edge of the rosebed. A large black purse! Maximus looked around to check there was no one else in the park. He picked it up. It felt quite heavy. There must be lots of money in it. He looked around again, just to make sure. Surely it wouldn't do any harm to see how much was in it?

It was full of ten pound notes. There must have been at least twenty of them. Maximus couldn't believe it. Two hundred pounds. He'd never seen so much in his life. Two hundred pounds would last him for weeks. He could buy more CDs. He might even manage to go to the next *Hard Cheese* gig. It was what he had always wanted – to see *Hard Cheese* and get their autographs. Maximus dropped the purse inside his empty Wasda bag.

He was rich. He was richer than he ever thought possible. Or was he? Was it his to keep? If *he* had found it, then *someone* had lost it. Fancy losing all that money. Of course it wouldn't be a problem if you had lots – but what if you didn't? What if this money was all someone had?

What should he do? He could go to Wasda and buy all those things he really loved – a big bag of ant-flavoured crisps, a piece of Cheddar cheese twice his own size, some wax waffles, some chocolate mousse and lots more. Or... he could give the purse back... hand it in at a police station.

Maximus started to cross the road towards Wasda. He was thinking so hard that he nearly got knocked over by two frogs on mountain bikes.

'Wake up, you dozy mouse!' shouted one of the frogs. 'Not safe out on your own, you aren't.'

Maximus ignored them. He took a trolley from the trolley park and walked in past the checkout. As he got nearer he heard some loud voices.

'You must pay for it,' said the girl hedgehog sitting at the checkout. 'If you can't pay then I shall have to get the Manager.'

Standing by the checkout and frantically searching her bag was an old duck. She was looking very worried and frightened. Her voice was quite quacked.

'But it was here. I know it was here,' she said. 'I never go out without my purse.'

'Well, where is it?' said the checkout hedgehog. Other animals in the queue were beginning to make noises. 'I can't keep all these customers waiting.'

'I don't know,' sobbed the duck. 'If I've lost it, then I've lost everything. All the money I have. I was taking it to the bank – to the River Bank.'

'I'm sorry you've lost your money,' said the girl hedgehog, 'but you'll just have to put all these things back where you got them from.'

The duck began to reload her trolley. Maximus stood there watching her. All that money belonged to her. She must have lost the purse when she came out of the park.

'It's... er, all right,' said Maximus, walking over to the checkout. He took the purse from his bag. 'I think this must be yours?'

'It would have been very easy to keep it,' said Maximus, later that day, to Patrick and Paula. 'But I am very glad I didn't.'

'How about supper with us?' asked Paula. 'We're having confetti soup and roast hymn book cover.'

Loving Father,
Sometimes we see things that don't belong to us and we want them. Help us to be honest in all things and remember that what doesn't belong to us does belong to someone else. Amen.

Breaking is taking

There was a loud bang and pieces of glass showered over Maximus. One moment he had been watching *Mouse Party* on television and the next he was scampering for his life under the vicar's desk.

He stood there with his whole body shaking and his whiskers twitching. He waited with his front paws covering his ears, but nothing else happened. He shook himself and began to remove the pieces of glass which had stuck in his fur.

Very slowly he came out from under the desk. There were pieces of glass all over the floor and Maximus had to pick his way through them. He headed for the door, crossed over the church, and knocked on the Sunday School cupboard.

'Whatever's the matter?' said a surprised looking Patrick.

Maximus was standing there shaking and holding his head.

'Come in. Paula... it's Maximus, he's been hurt.'

Paula came rushing in, took one look at Maximus, and got out her First Aid Kit. Maximus had two or three nasty cuts from the flying glass.

'Well, I don't think you need to go to hospital,' said Paula later. 'We've stopped the bleeding. Now, when you're ready, please tell us what happened.'

Maximus told them everything he knew – which wasn't very much. Something had broken the vestry window and he had been sitting where some of the glass had fallen.

'I think, when you're feeling OK, we'd better go and have a look,' said Patrick.

A few minutes later the three mice were in the vestry looking at the mess. There was a large hole in the window and lying on top of the vicar's desk was half a brick. The glass from the window had gone everywhere and walking about was very dangerous.

'Vandalism. Just vandalism,' said Patrick. 'Some stupid human thought it was clever to throw a brick through the church window.'

'Well, we can't do any more here. I think you'd better come and spend the night with us,' said Paula, putting a paw round Maximus' shoulder. 'I wouldn't want to think of you here on your own.'

Maximus didn't like to admit it, but he was very glad Paula had invited him. He was still very shaken and worried that whoever had thrown the brick might do it again. Besides which, the vicar would have to clear up the mess. There would be dust and glass and ladders and probably policemen. A small mouse was better off out of the way for a day or two.

The next morning, after the mouselings had gone to school, Patrick and Maximus went for a walk in the graveyard.

'It's a terrible thing to happen,' said Patrick, as they walked towards the churchyard gate. 'I just don't understand how humans can behave like that.'

'Oh no!' shouted Maximus. 'Look... over there.'

Standing near the gate was a large notice-board. It gave the times of services, the vicar's address and other important notices. The notice-board was covered in red and blue paint. The paint had dripped all over the board and run onto the ground. It was a terrible mess.

Just as the two mice were looking at the board the vicar came through the gate. He didn't see the mice but they saw him. He stopped and stared at the board. He shook his head and then ran up the path to the door which led into the vestry. In a very short time a policeman drove into the church car park. The mice saw the vicar showing the policeman the notice-board and the broken window.

'I'm sorry, but there isn't very much we can do,' said the policeman. 'There are people about who seem to think that vandalism is fun. They just don't care.'

'That window and the board will cost hundreds of pounds to repair,' said the vicar. 'Sadly, it will mean we can't do other things. Everyone will suffer because somebody thinks it's clever to spoil our church.'

'But it isn't just the window and the board,' said Patrick to Maximus. 'You might have been killed if the brick had fallen on you. As it is, you were cut and nearly scared out of your fur.'

'People just don't think,' said Maximus, 'about what might happen. They don't think that it will cost a lot of money to put things right. They don't respect what belongs to others.'

The mice spent the rest of the day watching new glass being put in the window. The broken glass was cleared up and the notice-board cleaned. It took a long time for everything to get back to normal and it was several days before Maximus felt happy about sleeping in the vestry again.

That Sunday all the mice hid in the church to hear what the vicar had to say.

'There has been some very serious damage done to our church,' he told the people. 'The window in the vestry was smashed and the notice-board ruined. It has cost a lot of money for repairs, money we were going to give to people who really needed it. It is hard for us to see this happen to our church.

'There are evil people about who do wrong things. They seem to think it is clever to spoil what belongs to others. They do not respect other people or the beautiful world that God has given us. We must pray for them and for ourselves that we take care of God's world. That is what he wants us to be... care-takers.'

'That's what I am,' said Maximus to himself, 'I'm the caretaker of this church.'

Heavenly Father,
We see many things that spoil your beautiful world –
it must make you very sad. Help us to respect what
belongs to others as we want others to respect what
belongs to us. Amen.

A is for All and S is for Share: Harvest

If there was one season that Maximus looked forward to more than any other, it was harvest. It was the time in the year when people brought lots of lovely food to church. They played a funny sort of game with him – they put the food in lots of different places. He had to chase all over the church to find what he wanted. Fruit was put on the window-sills, vegetables were laid round the pulpit, flowers filled vases to overflowing and often there was a sheaf of corn. There was a newly baked harvest loaf which had a wonderful whisker-twitching smell.

Maximus really looked forward to harvest. It wasn't only the adults who brought him lots of food. There was always a Family Service and the children brought baskets and boxes with even more. Maximus was very grateful to everyone but, even with Patrick and Paula and the mouselings, they could never eat it all.

Maximus always liked the harvest hymns. His favourite was 'All things bright and beautiful', because he was sure that the words *all creatures great and small* were about him. He didn't know who the great was but the small was definitely him.

Maximus had written his own verse to the hymn. It went like this:

'Each little mouse is grateful,
Just listen to them squeak.
So thank you everybody –
Can we have it every week?'

By the time the Family Service started, Maximus, Patrick, Paula and the mouselings had already eaten far more than they should. They had found delicious red apples by the organ, a banana on the pulpit, several ears of corn had now disappeared from the big sheaf and there was even a small piece missing from the special harvest loaf.

Maximus and the others always enjoyed Family Services and were usually somewhere hiding in the church listening and joining in. Harvest Festival was a must, and they were all there, including the thirty-four mouselings. They sang the hymns, listened to the prayers and Bible readings and waited for the vicar to speak.

'Harvest is a wonderful time,' he said. 'It is a time when we come to church and say thank you to God for all the good things he has given us. Some people think that harvest is only about food.'

'Well, of course it is,' whispered Maximus to Patrick. 'That's why I think harvest is best.'

'But,' went on the vicar, 'it is much more than that. At harvest we do say "thank you" to God but we do it for many reasons. I wonder if one of the children would come out and spell "harvest" for me?'

All the mouselings put their paws in the air but of course the vicar didn't see them.

'Right, Louise, how does it go?' said the vicar.

'H, A, R, V, E, S, T,' she said.

'Quite right,' said the vicar. 'Now, please hold this card.'

On the card was a large letter H.

'H stands for our HOMES. We thank God at harvest that we have homes. Homes that are warm and clean and comfortable. Homes where we can be part of a loving family.'

The vicar gave cards to other children when they came out and they held them up for everyone to see.

'R stands for RECREATION. That's a big word meaning play and games and holidays and having fun and enjoying yourself. We thank God at harvest that we can do these things.

'V stands for VEGETABLES. We may not always like eating green cabbage but we have lots of vegetables and fruit to enjoy. Look around the church and you will see apples and bananas, carrots and cabbage, and many more. You know, I think our church mice enjoy them too – I've noticed some small bites in some of the fruit.'

Maximus and the others looked very embarrassed when the vicar said this.

'We have so much food in this country and we really don't know what it is to be hungry. We thank God at harvest for all the food he gives us.

'E stands for EDUCATION. Louise came out to the front and spelt the word HARVEST for us. She was able to do that because she has been to school and learnt to read. We enjoy many things in our lives because of our education – because we can read and write and understand numbers. At harvest we thank God for our education and for all those who teach us.

'T stands for THANKS. At harvest we come to say a very big "thank you" to God for all the wonderful things that he gives us – our homes, our recreation, our food and our education.'

The mouselings started chattering. Paula asked them to be quiet.

'But Mum,' said Posy, 'the vicar can't spell. He's missed out two letters.'

'Sh... listen,' said Paula, 'perhaps he hasn't finished.'

'So that's what our letters stand for,' the vicar continued. 'But H, R, V, E, T don't spell harvest. There are two letters missing. They are special letters. A stands for ALL and S stands for SHARE.

'At harvest we shouldn't just think of ourselves. We should think of ALL people everywhere. We should think of those who have no homes, who cannot play because they are ill, those who never have enough to eat and those who have no schools to go to. It's those with whom we should SHARE our harvest.

'As you know, your gifts of food and fruit will be shared with people nearby. Your gifts of money will be used to help those in other countries who do not have a good harvest. As we thank God at harvest for what we have, so we pray for those who have very little.'

'There's more to harvest than I ever thought,' said Maximus to Patrick after the service. 'I must remember those letters.'

Loving Father,
You give us so much – our food, our homes, our schools, our play and the love of those who care for us. Help us to remember that many people are hungry or homeless, have no schools or play. Help us to show them your love by caring for them. Amen.

'There's nothing alive in there': Easter

It was a perfect autumn day. Maximus and Patrick were enjoying the sunshine as they sat on a stone in the churchyard. Flying just above them were several butterflies, their wings catching the sun. Suddenly Maximus started to wriggle.

'Got an itch, Maximus?' asked Patrick laughing.

'There's something in my fur on my back,' said Maximus. 'I can't quite reach it.' He squirmed again.

'It's a caterpillar,' said Patrick. 'A little green caterpillar. Poor thing must think it's in the jungle!'

Patrick gently took the caterpillar from Maximus' fur and put it down on the stone. The mice laughed as it hunched its back and crawled away.

'Amazing things, caterpillars and butterflies,' said Patrick. 'I mean, you and I grew inside our mothers and then we were born in a warm nest. But with butterflies it's different.'

'Look,' said Maximus. He was pointing to a bush that grew by the churchyard wall. 'I've just seen some butterflies land on that. I wonder what they're doing?'

The mice went closer to the bush. It was full of furry caterpillars – lots and lots of them, all chewing the leaves. As well as the caterpillars there were eggs, laid by the butterflies, hanging down from some of the smaller stems of the bush. As they watched, one of the eggs opened, and a tiny caterpillar wriggled out.

'It's amazing – really amazing,' said Patrick.

'But what happens now?' asked Maximus. 'I mean, it'll be winter soon. Won't the caterpillars just die?'

'I don't think so. For the next few weeks they will eat as many leaves as they can. They'll grow much bigger and then they turn into pupae.'

'Into what?' asked Maximus.

'Pupae. It's a bit like you snuggling down under your duvet so no-one knows there is a mouse under it. The caterpillar lives inside this sort of sleeping-bag for weeks. Another name for a pupa is chrysalis.'

'And it stays there all through the winter?'

'Yes, some pupae will do that. Anyway, it's time I went home. Paula's cooking some pages of organ music for supper. She says organic food is better for you.'

The weather turned cold and Maximus and Patrick didn't go out into the graveyard very often.

One day, Maximus saw a strange thing hanging from one of the dried flower stems in the vestry. It was brown and looked a bit like a tiny sock. It seemed to be very dead and uninteresting. He was pulling it off the stem when Patrick came in.

'Don't do that,' said his friend. 'That's what we were talking about weeks ago. It's a pupa or chrysalis. There's a butterfly waiting to come out when the weather's better.'

'What a load of rubbish,' said Maximus. 'Pull the other paw! That's dead. There's nothing alive in there.'

'Well, if you don't believe me, watch what happens.'

Time went on. The days began to grow longer and lighter again. Maximus kept an eye on the chrysalis but nothing much seemed to happen.

'It's dead,' he said to Patrick just before Easter. 'Nothing's going to happen.'

On Easter Day the mice went to the Family Service. There were lots of people there singing the hymns about Jesus coming back to life again.

'A very happy Easter to you all,' said the vicar.

'And to you too,' squeaked the mouselings politely.

'Today is a wonderful day,' continued the vicar. 'It's the day that Jesus was seen alive again by some of his friends. I wonder how they felt? They knew he had died on the day we call Good Friday. They knew he had been buried in a grave. They must have been terribly sad and unhappy thinking they would never see him again. Of course not everyone believed that he was alive again. One of Jesus' friends called Thomas said, "I won't believe it until I see Jesus myself." And very soon after that he did see Jesus and he did believe it.'

After the service, Maximus invited Patrick, Paul and the mouselings back to the vestry.

'I've got a surprise for you,' he told the mouselings. The mouselings followed Maximus into the vestry and he gave each of them a tiny chocolate Easter egg.

'Maximus,' said Patrick, 'I've got a surprise for you too. Look over there.' Patrick pointed to the window-sill. There, in the warm sun, was the most beautiful butterfly. Maximus rushed over to where the chrysalis had been hanging. It was cracked and empty. What had seemed dead had come alive again.

'That is just amazing,' said Maximus. 'Happy Easter everyone.'

Heavenly Father,
Thank you that Easter Day follows Good Friday –
that Jesus came back to life again. Help us to live as
those who love a living saviour – Jesus Christ. Amen.